Stay

D1025350

bitlit

A **free** eBook edition is available
with the purchase of this print book.

CLEARLY PRINT YOUR NAME ABOVE IN UPPER CASE

Instructions to claim your free eBook edition:
1. Download the BitLit app for Android or iOS
2. Write your name in **UPPER CASE** on the line
3. Use the BitLit app to submit a photo
4. Download your eBook to any device

Stay

KATHERINE LAWRENCE

COTEAU BOOKS

© Katherine Lawrence, 2017

All rights reserved. No part of this publication may be reproduced, stored in a retrieval system or transmitted, in any form or by any means, without the prior written consent of the publisher or a licence from The Canadian Copyright Licensing Agency (Access Copyright). For an Access Copyright licence, visit www.accesscopyright.ca or call toll free to 1-800-893-5777.

This book is a work of fiction. Names, characters, places and incidents either are the products of the author's imagination or are used fictitiously. Any resemblance to actual persons, living or dead, is coincidental.

Edited by Alice Major
Book designed by Tania Craan
Typeset by Susan Buck
Printed and bound in Canada

Library and Archives Canada Cataloguing in Publication

Lawrence, Katherine, 1955-, author
        Stay / Katherine Lawrence.

Issued in print and electronic formats.
ISBN 978-1-55050-681-5 (softcover).--ISBN 978-1-55050-682-2 (PDF).--
ISBN 978-1-55050-683-9 (EPUB).--ISBN 978-1-55050-684-6 (Kindle)

        I. Title.

PS8623.A9265S73 2017   jC813'.6   C2016-907043-3
                                                C2016-907044-1

Library of Congress Control Number   2016957176

2517 Victoria Avenue
Regina, Saskatchewan
Canada S4P 0T2
www.coteaubooks.com

Available in Canada from:
Publishers Group Canada
2440 Viking Way
Richmond, British Columbia
Canada V6V 1N2

Available in the US from:
Orca Book Publishers
www.orcabook.com
1-800-210-5277

10 9 8 7 6 5 4 3 2 1

Coteau Books gratefully acknowledges the financial support of its publishing program by: the Saskatchewan Arts Board, The Canada Council for the Arts, the Government of Saskatchewan through Creative Saskatchewan, the City of Regina. We further acknowledge the [financial] support of the Government of Canada. Nous reconnaissons l'appui [financier] du gouvernement du Canada.

for Anna and Rachel

Table of Contents

Halo Hello

i.
My twin is buried in a wooden box
lined with white silk
soft as dandelion fluff, the stuff I blow
to the wind, to you,
                    Billy
it's me, Millie, your weather girl reporting graveside
about the latest family squall.
Did you hear the storm last night?

Yells of thunder from Dad, lightning in Mum's voice,
flash of tempers followed by silence—
sudden crack that jolted me upright: Mum wants
    a divorce.

Tears like rain — his, hers, mine. I listened for Tara
but our big sister is deaf to everything but her
    own playlist.

Billy, some nights I hide under blankets,
wish we were twinned in one bunk, tucked away
far away, riding that wild wave,
a roller coaster heave-ho that swooshed me
nine minutes head first *toodle-oo adios au revoir*
your fist the knuckles at the back of my knee,
the two of us a tangled knot of legs hands toes—

I held my breath as the doctor slapped my back,
cried for you, little brother,
but you didn't open your mouth,
didn't fill your lungs
with air.

Billy, you are the sun,
no ordinary star.

Hey, perk up. There's chocolate cake in our future.
We're eleven going on twelve next month.
My legs longer than my jeans,
feet fast as jackrabbits.

ii.
And you, Billy? Have you wings?
Can you text me from heaven?
Halo, hello.

C'mon, let's ride 'em bronco, hop on my bike.
I'll stuff the soccer ball in my basket
race down Webster's Hill
over the foot bridge near the cemetery.

Do you feel the wild grasses tickle my bare ankles?
Hear crickets hum the air? Look
I can see your headstone from the bridge
if I balance both my feet on the seat like a trick rider
rodeo queen (wearing a stoopid helmet).

Question: Do you get goose bumps when I trace
your stone letters?
WILLIAM 'BILLY' PATTERSON.
Me too.

Guess what? Nobody knows how often
we practice my kick—
knock knock soccer ball bounce—your headstone
a goalie from the other side.

Fines Accumulating Daily

Our house is a library, books
spilling off shelves, leaning

towers of fact and fiction
encyclopedia sneezing dust—*Ahchoo!*

Dad reads science with a pipe full of tobacco,
Mum drags history to bed.

Tara's addicted to vampires, blood
dripping soft-cover horrors.

I prefer to read family mysteries,
mother's text messages, sent

and received, her cell
a table of contents.

Snooping? Spying?
Try and stop me.

How else can I figure out
why Dad moved to the basement.

His bed the scratchy green couch
beside a furnace that snores.

Sent

Darling,
I'm running out of patience.
Michael refuses to move out of the basement.
How much longer can I keep you a secret?
xox

In

Sweetheart,
He's putting in time until he can find an apartment.
I went through the same thing, remember?
Stay beautiful, beautiful.
Love you.
x

Punctuation

I've got
the longest
ponytail
in class,
a blond
question
mark
curling
my
spine.

If my hair
could ask,
would Mum
brush
and comb
the answer?

Sweep my suspicions
into an updo?

Or braid
and tie
another lie?

Stop Asking Me Questions (1)

Billy, you're in my head and you're making it hurt.
Would a kiss help?
Go. To. Sleep.
Why don't Mum and Dad kiss goodnight anymore?
Who cares.
You?
If I kiss the air will you go to sleep?
Ok
    (kiss kiss)
You still awake?
I think Mum kisses somebody new.
Let's tell Dad.
Billy!
I'm asleep.

Jane

Jane runs up the steps to my front door
every morning knock knock ding-dong.

We walk to school together, arms
a chain fence linked at the elbow.

She's the desk I sit behind,
long black hair I pencil curl,
the raspberry popsicle we lickety split
on the walk back home to my house,
genius Jane conjuring up a costume
for Halloween: witch, beatnik, Cruella DeVille?

Last year she was pig-tailed Dorothy,
Toto's leash in hand, a collar around my neck.
How do we top Oz?

We need brain food, says Jane.

To a blender add:
2 scoops double chocolate ice cream
2 cups milk
1 cup raspberry yogurt
1 banana
1 teaspoon vanilla extract
Whir on high.
Pour and serve.
Slurp, burp,
wipe your mouth on your sleeve.

Cross-legged in my bedroom closet,
flashlight, pillows.
Jane's spoon dangles spit-stuck
from her tongue,
I tie our shoelaces together,
pretend twins, tangled feet.
Whohabeahahun, says Jane.
Huh?
She unglues her tongue:
Two heads are better than one.

We kick off our runners
work like Cinderella's mice,
brushing, combing back-to-back
our heads fused at the crown,

a single braid
streaming between our shoulder blades,
black blond black blond black thick blond,
two of Dad's white shirts
sleeves rolled above the elbow
buttons
winked and closed.

And in the hall mirror,
ooh-ah
Siamese twins for Halloween
each step, every breath
one.

Stop Asking Me Questions (2)

No Billy, you and I were not Siamese twins.
Do you love Jane better than me?
Chocolate milkshakes are the only thing I love
more than you.
Why?
'Cause chocolate tastes like heaven.
Hey, that's where I am.
That's where Mum says you are but I don't believe her.
You don't think I live in chocolate?
You live here, in my heart, where I talk to you
any time I want.
Why?
You live here, in my heart, where I can
STOP ANSWERING YOUR QUESTIONS
ANY TIME I WANT.

Trick or Treat

Ghosts howl on our street but a yowl rattles the moon,
something dead or near-dying, a wounded cry.
We ditch loot bags in the bushes, shake our braid loose,
unbutton white shirts and slip undone, unnoticed
from the last house, no longer one but two plus two
feet tracking a creature-call that draws
us like true north, every hair on my skin
alert, run a moonlight path, its golden glow leading
to a house hidden by weeds, a fence of pick-up sticks,
the night air whimpering, shivering.

No tricks, no magic, nothing
we can do for a skin-and-bone dog, nothing
in the sacs we ditched but red licorice, jaw breakers,
suckers, bubble gum, *apples*, whispers Billy
apples! I yell to Jane, and back we run
to the bushes, fill our pockets with juicy reds,
granny smith green, worry out loud:
Do dogs eat apples?
He barks, snarls when he hears us again,
strains against his chain
quiets
as we lawn bowl apples he catches in his jaw,
chomps, slobbers, swallows
licks leftover bits from his paws,
sniffs a damp circle on the ground.

Stop Asking Me Questions (3)

Millie, you awake?
No
I feel dog breath on the back of my neck. Do you?
No
I smell apples. Do you?
No
Was that the best Halloween of your life?
Argh
You and Jane were brave to phone the animal shelter.
Oh Billy, I can't stop thinking about that poor mutt.
Will somebody at the animal shelter give him a name?
Good question.
I've got lots more.

No Return Address

Next morning, we're greeted by a chorus of yelps,
barks, woofs! stink of dog pee and sawdust,
but we don't care
we've driven to the animal shelter, found
row B, cage #23, the pooch we saved.

"Hey Slim," says the lady who led us inside,
a shelter worker in rubber boots and a ball cap
key ring in one hand, chart in the other.

Slim cowers in the shadows,
brown coat dull as dead grass, four dirty white
socks, red collar of open sores from the chain
that lanced as he strained.

Jane squeezes her eyes shut, covers her mouth,
her voice a trapped animal. I hold her hand
like Dad holds mine; we're three soldiers
fighting back tears.

Slim doesn't wag his tail, doesn't
move closer to our bodies,
eyes are broken windows
black, empty.

"*Why?*" I ask no one, anyone, someone.
Who would turn a pet into a parcel of bones,
no return address?
"*Why?*"
The lady in the ball cap reads from her chart:
mixed breed, possible Labrador-Boxer cross
approximately two years old, female,
found chained to a tree,
no food, no water,
no sign of an owner.

I feel Dad's hand grip my shoulder, try
to steer me away, but I shrug him off,
slip my fingers from Jane's hand to my pocket,
feel for the apple slice I tucked away,
push the treat between two cold metal bars, quick
before anyone can tell me *stop!*
Slim sniffs at sweetness, looks
from the apple to me.

Tail thumps. Just once.

They Finally Agree on Something

I'd walk her every day.
No, says Mum.
I'd stoop and scoop.
No, says Dad.
I'd train her not to chew.
No, says Mum.
But why?
The timing is bad, says Dad.
The timing for what? I ask.
For this family, says Mum.

I look to Dad, his shoulders slump—
I wish
with all my heart
I wish
I had an apple
in my pocket
for Dad.

Sent

I don't want to be home while Michael packs.

In

I'll book a room and wait for you in the lobby.
Scared?

Sent

Not when I'm with you.

In

Love you.
xxx

Secret Agent

I polish a dark keyhole in the mist
of my bedroom window
spot Dad outside beside the car,
trunk lid open,
street light directing suitcases,
blankets, books, the old vacuum cleaner,
pots and pans, desk chair,
watch him climb behind the wheel,
pull away from the curb, drive so slow
I could jog beside him, ask where's he's going
but he turns at the corner, leaves a grey trail
of smoke that lingers in the night air,
fades away.

Divorce

Mum flips Sunday waffles
on a school morning,
tries to buttermilk Tara and me
about new arrangements—
                      we'll live with Dad
every second weekend at his new apartment.

Tara stabs a strawberry with her fork.
I drag my bacon
through a puddle of maple syrup,
chew and swallow.

I Spy

in Dad's bedroom closet
on the shelf he stacks sweaters
a framed photograph:
me in diapers and sun hat, Tara
posed with red pail and shovel
our teen Mum in a teenie weenie
white bikini, her smile wide
as the umbrella
planted in the sand.

Sent

I start full-time next week.
My first lucky break in ages.
See you at lunch.
Love you.
P.S.
You can be teacher's pet.

In

Congratulations, teacher!
Adore you.
xx

A Call to the Animal Shelter

Billybillybillybillybilly
I've got good news, bad news
bad news, good news she's
gonegonegonegonegone
somebody adopted Slim but I'm not her
somebodysomebodysomebody.

Dad Behind the Ears

Mum says nothing will change.
Same house, same school.
She says, *Stop being so melodramatic*
caught me in the bathroom dabbing
Dad's after-shave
behind my ears,
a glass bottle forgotten
on his side of the cupboard
cinnamon-vanilla, hint of boot leather,
the everyday of my dad:
his whistle while he shaved,
specks of black beard peppering
the sink basin,
helping him choose a tie:
red plaid, diagonal stripes, daisy dots
picked by the girl whose throat
is now a Windsor knot.

Cemetery Dream

Do the coyotes that leave footprints in the snow
sleep with you, Billy?

I gather blossoms of their golden fur, squat and study
white hammocks matted with animal dreams.

Do the coyotes keep you warm, Billy?

I cry for Dad when I wake cold in the night, the sound
of his step at my door is a blanket I sleep without.

New Math

Four chairs at the kitchen table minus one Dad equals
an empty place I can't subtract from the meals we ate
together, Dad's clown-around jokes, holding a banana
to his ear like a telephone, his direct line *to those monkeys
in Ottawa* or serving our Friday night specialty—
Chicken à la Daddy—deep fried and golden, Mum's
pink apron tied around his middle, white chef's hat from
the dollar store perched on his head, Tara, Mum and
me pretending we're part of a TV cooking show called
One Dish Dad, his studio audience laughing for real.

It's my job to set the table every night for dinner but
I hate the new math in our house: three plates, three
glasses, three forks, three spoons, knife knife knife.

Sent

Hey Lover,
Thinking about your invitation.
Michael has the kids that weekend so I'm a free woman.
What can I bring to the cabin?
xo

In

Sweetie,
Just pack your woolies. The weekend is my treat.
Love you.
xxx

Me Me Me

I can't believe that Mother said *yes*
when I asked for a birthday party,
noon until midnight, twelve divine hours

with my twelve favourite best friends.
What if she changes her mind?
I can't believe that Mother said *yes*

Too bad, so sad, I'd tell her.
The invitations are presto! gone,
noon until midnight, twelve hilarious hours

I've planned a scavenger hunt,
charades, two bowling lanes that glow
I can't believe that Mother said *yes*

We'll barbeque hamburgers, share
dill pickle ripple chips, angel food cake
noon to midnight, twelve delicious hours

Everyone will sing to me me *me*
fa so la te do, close my eyes, make a wish,
I can't believe that Mother said *yes*
Noon to midnight, twelve short hours.

In

How about dinner with the guy who loves you?
xx

Sent

Full-time work and Millie's birthday party
have knocked the stuffing out of me.
We'll catch up at the cabin.
Miss you.

Three Simple Words

How many times did I walk past
the small narrow sign
glued hard as law
to the front door
of Dad's apartment?
First time when he moved in last month.
Did I read the sign? No.
Second when he cooked *Chicken à la Daddy*
without Mum's pink apron or his chef's hat.
Did I read the sign? No.
Third time today after school.
Did I read the sign? No.
I have eyes, I can read.
But I didn't (or maybe I refused)
until Dad led me by the hand
after telling me *no no no*
told me to open my eyes and R.E.A.D:
NO DOGS ALLOWED
I stood outside the apartment door,
read and re-read,
stuck my fingers in my ears
my face a river of snivel.

Listen, Billy

Funny, not ha-ha funny just weird funny how I started crying at Dad's crummy apartment and couldn't stop. I paused long enough to eat a bite of grilled cheese sandwich for supper but then I started as soon as I climbed into bed. I cried myself to sleep like a big baby. I don't understand why he and Mum have to live in two separate places because it means I can't have a dog. Mum says she's too busy working as a teacher to look after a dog, especially every second weekend when I'd have to leave the dog with her because of course, of course! NO DOGS ALLOWED at Dad's dumb apartment. Mum says I'm a selfish girl. Dad says he wishes things were different but I don't believe him. If he wanted to make everything different he'd make our family the same again. And then I could have a dog. Everybody under the same roof. But he says Mum doesn't love him anymore so I better get used to living in two places. When I asked why she doesn't love him he got that sad look in his eyes that made me wish I could slap a plate of waffles in front of him, cheer him up the way Sunday breakfast always used to make him happy.

Billy, if Mum fell out of love with Dad, do you think that she can fall out of love with me? With Tara? Would she pack away the small glass angel that sleeps in her china cabinet? Is love like a tree leaf that turns brown and drops to the ground? If I had a dog, I would love my puppy evergreen.

Boom Times

A new boy in our class from Newfoundland,
Jimmy York, his accent so peculiar strange
everybody elbowed near
to hear him talk
icebergs, humpback whales
a boat named Dory. His father
drove eight days across the Trans-Canada,
St. John's to Saskatoon with Jimmy,
his mum, four little sisters and a guinea pig
named Puffin, parked the crew
at his auntie's house,
then left for a job mining uranium
way up north in black bear country.
It's a modern gold rush out here, says Jimmy,
but us from away can't hardly finds
a place to live.

Jimmy got me thinking
how I've got one bed too many
while he's got none, says he sleeps
on a bedroll in auntie's living room,
Puffin caged and nibbling hard
wooden blocks from sunset to sunrise.

Dear City Council,

The first black president of the United States, Barack Obama, let his daughters, Malia and Sasha, have a puppy *in the White House*. Elected officials do not own property; they rent.

I have read that Rachel and Ben Harper, the children of a former Canadian prime minister, lived with a bunch of rescue cats in their official residence at 24 Sussex Drive, Ottawa. I think it is good to give dogs and cats a warm, safe home.

However, I do not think that it is fair that the kids of famous politicians get to have pets in *their* RENTAL houses but that I, Millicent Helen Patterson, am not allowed the same rights and privileges at my father's apartment.

I have some political pet-facts to share with you. William Lyon Mackenzie King, the longest serving prime minister in our history, had a dog named Pat who gave him political advice. British Prime Minister Winston Churchill adopted several orange cats and named every one of them Jock. Churchill may have lacked imagination but he was dedicated to cats. I admire his compassion.

I also know that kings and queens have kept animals in castles—*rental* castles. King Henry III kept three leopards, a white bear and an elephant in the Tower of London. Queen Elizabeth II keeps Corgi dogs in Buckingham Palace.

I am not famous. I am not a member of a royal family. I am a Canadian school girl (and a twin) who believes that all children have a right to own a pet even when their parents rent an apartment.

Respectfully yours—

Silver Lining

We're not best friends, my sister and me
but at Dad's we share a bedroom, whisper
across our twin beds, double-up for warmth.
We're not best friends, my sister and me.

Tara wants to run away from home.
Which one? I ask, making her laugh.
We're not best friends, my sister and me,
But at Dad's we share a bedroom, whisper.

Stop Asking Me Questions (4)

Where have you been?
I've been busy, Billy.
Too busy for me?
Busy learning a new bus route. Busy hauling my
suitcase between Mum's house and Dad's apartment.
You don't like living at Dad's?
It's hard for me to remember all the stuff I need to
pack and re-pack every week.
What more do you need than pajamas?
Two pairs of running shoes, two pencil cases, an extra
winter coat, a piano.
A piano?
I can only practice my songs when I'm at Mum's.
You wish you could practice Frosty the Snowman more often?
That's the one good thing about the divorce.
*Brain wave: If I was alive Mum and Dad would have to
buy us double stuff. You think that means I saved them
money by dying before I was born?*
Brain wave: Maybe I should tell them to treat me like a
twin, buy me two of everything.
Two bicycles?
For sure.
Two pairs of soccer cleats?
Totally.
You think we're going to end up with two dads?
That guy Mum goes out with stinks like garlic.
How about two mums?

Oh Billy, I wish I hadn't found those black high heel shoes under Dad's bed last week.

What were you snooping for?

My slippers, the ones trimmed with white fur.

Ya, you need two of everything.

Not two mums and two dads, Billy.

That would be our worst case scenario, right?

A nightmare.

Dog Names Don't Visit Me Anymore

don't collect in the margins of school books,
ink my palms, doodle scratch pads,
a constellation of twinkling eyes,
floppy ears, tails and pink tongues
drinking from the Big Dipper:
> *Cocoa, Suzanna, Zephyr*
> *Cookie, Angel, Pluto.*

I used to hope on birthdays, Christmas,
wishbones, falling stars, rainy days alone
with a sheet of paper
catching names like rain drops:
> *Caramel, Puddles, Whiffle.*

Imagined the bowl of kibble I'd have ready,
fresh water, the old red sleeping bag,
collar, leash and a name from the list
I rip, twist, pitch at my suitcase, the constant
companion named Baggage.

Sent

Darling,
Sorry I couldn't meet you for lunch but Michael didn't
show.
I waited at the lawyer's for an hour.
I am steamed.

In

Sweetie,
I figured you got delayed by either traffic or Millie.
Poor you.
Two more weeks until the cabin.
Love you,
xxxxx

Uncaged

Jimmy brought Puffin to school in a cookie tin
lined with wood shavings pale as Jimmy's face,
a sad show 'n' tell at lunch,
limp small body, butterscotch brown.
Our circle of friends took turns, no shoving,
Puffin's black eyes shut against fingers
hands, Jimmy's lips.

Victor and Terri offered to dig a hole
under the red swings,
Twyla said we could bundle old Puffin
in her blue wool scarf, Jane insisted
we work fast before rigor mortis set in.

Rigor who? asked Jimmy.
So Jane performed, staged a fall
collapsed, kicked once, went stiff
as a stick.
Jimmy's cheeks dimpled
two rosy dots, pulled Jane to her feet.

My pig don't want nothin'
to do with a school yard cemetery.

Jimmy tucked Puffin back into bed,
pressed the lid tight while all of us stood
silent in the windless noon.

Billy at School

You pester me all afternoon in class,
turn pages in my mind so fast
I lose my place inside the space
of long division, extra homework.

Your whispers fill my ears,
Can't hear Mrs. Hanley over your
questions: *What time does class end?*
What does a dead pig look like?
What killed Puffin?

I scribble answers to you, head down,
pencil and paper props to make Mrs. Hanley
believe I'm working hard, paying attention
as I write answers to my twin:
The bell rings at 3:20 p.m.
A dead pig looks like a dead pig.
Puffin died of old age.

After school, I lead Jimmy and the gang
to a grassy place near your gravesite, kneel
cold knees and dig with our rulers,
fingers, arrow-sharp rocks, place a beloved pig
close to you, Billy, leader of our guinea pack.

Neighbourhood Gossip

1. Twyla Harvey's father moved back home after Mrs. Harvey told him she was going to have a baby.

2. Victor MacKay has one father and three mothers: his birth mother, his mother's partner and his father's wife.

3. Sammy Johnson's mother told him if anyone asks about his sister, he's to say nobody's beeswax.

4. Jimmy York's mother wears fancy panties made from a piece of skinny black string.

5. Terri Turner will be her mother's bridesmaid next summer for the second time. Terri gets to wear the green strapless dress again.

6. Mandy Wickerton's father left home to live in a trailer with a blond lady the same age as Mandy's big sister.

7. David Pomroy's mother kissed David's father smack in the middle of the street.

8. Emma Twillinger's mother hurled the sugar bowl at Emma's father last night so nobody had any sugar to sprinkle on porridge in the morning.

9. Millie Patterson's mother has a boyfriend with an

eye in the middle of his forehead, scales on his skin, thick yellow toenails.

10. Millie Patterson's father was seen walking out of the Sutton Cancer Clinic last week.

Vanilla Snow

My throat is a forest on fire,
Tara's cigarette a bribe
I should have doused.

I inhaled like she showed me,
choked on smoke, burned
a hole in the promise
I made to Mum and Dad,
their old pack-a-day habits.

Next time Tara sneaks home
past midnight I'll demand
vanilla ice cream cold as snow.

Ghost

I miss the ghost who haunted our house,
a phantom pickpocket robber thief
blamed by Mum for whatever went missing—
(scissors, ruler, dustpan, hairbrush)
couldn't find—
(tweezers, pliers, masking tape)
She'd say
   Must be that ghost again.

Now Dad's the spook she blames
for what's no longer here—
(desk lamp, filing cabinet
The Oxford English Dictionary,
cheese grater, pizza knife)
stuff she replaces on shopping trips.
But she never buys old newspapers,
or a reading chair with salted
peanuts under the cushion.

Dollars and Sense

Money buys nothing but fights, arguments, phone
calls, silence cold as my bare feet (forgot slippers at
Dad's, left my green hoodie in the closet.)

Mum says she can't afford two of everything, won't
waste gas driving back to the apartment for clothes. I
need to learn my lesson, Tara too: science book, soccer
jersey, the cost of falling out of love.

Payola

Tara scores top marks, even her excuses
are clever, her mind designs logical, plausible
reasons for not going to Dad's after school:
    Friday night drama rehearsals,
    band practice, cramps
while I'm stuck at the apartment alone,
three TV channels, cards, a balcony playpen.

Tara arrived at Dad's after dark (again)
threw her make-up bag at my head (missed)
when I mentioned payola, she owed me
for shutting up about what I spied
at home: Jason Greenwood and Tara
on the couch k-i-s-s-i-n-g
first comes love, then comes marriage
then comes Tara with a baby carriage,
Jason's bare feet big as the secret
Tara expects me to keep
for one tube of mascara,
a bottle of nail polish purple
as the icky hicky on her neck.

Playing Baseball

I got smacked in the gut
winded, same crack
I heard gathering speed

all those years

I thought I was home safe.
My parents a white leather ball,
their decision hard and fast.

Saturday Afternoon

Jane and Jimmy meet me at Dad's park.
Snow angels, snow babies, chase clouds
shaped like poodles, terriers, an Irish Wolfhound,
our hearts off-leash, sun dogs in the sky.

Sunday Morning

Awake but scared to open my eyes—
daylight might chase away
the first name I've dreamed
in a long time:
Sky, a blond pup
tugging the end of a kite string
front paws white as daisy petals,
eyes double-yellow bright.

In

One more sleep and you're mine
for the weekend.
Sweet dreams my love.

Sent

I'm packed and (almost) ready!
Love you, lover.

Miss Berry Wants New Information

current data
for every student,
gave us yellow forms
to take home, sign and return.

I read what I could
then understood
I'd need extra lines
for two addresses,
more phone numbers
than a telephone book
an explanation
about bus pick-up one week
but not the next.

I folded the page, stuffed it
into my locker like a stale
ham sandwich.

The Journey

i) Not Invited

*Liver*boy drove us to Dad's,
one hand on the wheel,
the other draped around Mum's shoulder,
bug-black hair crawling his knuckles,
my skin an itchy wool sweater.

A cardboard box sat obediently
as a well-trained dog between Tara and me:
wine bottles, CDs, a bag of salted cashews.
Help yourself, he said, winking at us
in the rearview mirror.

We both said *no thank you*
pretended
we're allergic to nuts.

ii) Apartment Keys

Tara policed her pockets
rang buzzer #1406 again, again
dead air.
Figured Dad was at the lab, rattling
test tubes, weighing, measuring
new varieties of chickpeas, black beans
lentils for prairie farmers.

He's just like Tara, brilliant but absent-minded—
loses socks, hats, keys, forgets
anniversaries, birthdays, Mother's Day,
appointments with teachers, bankers, lawyers.

Mum's mind is a computer
though once I heard her on the phone
admit she couldn't remember
why she ever married Dad.

iii) Bus Tickets

Tara smacked the front door with her fist
said *Let's go home*
threw an orange bus ticket at me
stomped off, wouldn't wait.
Had to zipper my backpack, struggle
straps over my shoulders
What's the big hurry?

I shadowed her to a bus,
asked for a *transfer please*
just like Tara, walked past empty seats
to the back.
Everything she did, I did too,
except say hi to
Jason *Worm*wood.

iv) Don't Be A Baby

Tara told me I was old enough
to go home by myself,
she and Jason wanted to ride
downtown to a movie. All I had to do
was get off across from *hereandnow*,
transfer to bus *somethingorother*, ring the bell
at *comeandgo corner*, catch *I forget*
and watch for the red mailbox.
    Simple, said Jason as he leaned
into Tara, the bus hugging
a shoulder, slowing to a stop.

I watched from the bus window
as my sister and her stupid boyfriend
blended into strangers on the street.
Then I stood up, pulled down
the bell cord,
my head ringing.

v) Downtown

No way could I find Tara, spot her jean jacket, dark
blond ponytail, Jason's black ball cap, couldn't think
what to do, the crowd a mind of its own. I kept walking, backpack bouncing, watched for movie theatres,
Tara and Jason in line, maybe they stopped for a ham-
burger, fries, then caught my reflection in a fast food
window: Lost. Crossed and moved on, past T-Shirt
Shack, Tattoo Alley, Sip 'n' Chat, Sears where once
Mum and I bought Dad a tie maybe I could try the
men's department, beg a salesman for help; *don't be a
baby*, watched for green lights, for Dad, for Tara, a
teacher, a neighbour, a shopping mall with a pay phone
inside the entrance, dropped my backpack, rummaged
my pencil case for coins, dialed the apartment—no
answer, phoned home—no answer, tried Mum on her
cell: her answer a fire alarm.

vi) Parents Work in Mysterious Ways

Waited while other people used the pay phone,
waited while a girls' soccer team burst into the mall,
waited while the same team left wearing new hoodies,
waited while my stomach grumbled for fries with gravy,
waited while the mall lights brightened as the sky darkened,
waited while my backpack doubled as a lumpy bench,
waited until my Dad—
                              Dad? Dad!
hugged me hard, kept saying *sorrysorrysorry* as we drove
home to my house, Mum at the front window—
                                        no wave, no smile.

This is my fault, said Dad. *I didn't remember it was Friday*.
I knew better than to ask what day of the week Dad
thought it was, or what became of Mum's getaway
weekend with *Liver*boy.

vii) Family Meal

First time in a long time
we've eaten supper at home together,
everyone in their own seat,
Mum picking coins of meat off her pizza
Dad eating the extra pepperoni
said he forgot about her weekend plans,
said sorry with his eyes.
Me too, I'm sorry I got off the bus,
Tara said she was sorry she went to a movie,
sorrier that Jason doesn't drive a car,
wiped her mouth on her sleeve,
stood up from the table and said *goodnight*
but Mum said *no*
we were going home with Dad,
she needed time alone
had papers to mark.

viii) Back to Dad's

I wonder how Mum would like moving
back and forth every second
weekend. All the stuff
in my head I need to say out loud
but some words are at Dad's
others at Mum's, my sentences scattered
between two homes
like a trail of socks that don't match.

Heart's Desire

I'd like to sell our house, buy
a duplex with two doors,
two floors and a plaster wall dividing Mum
from Dad; live together
in a house designed like a heart:
two chambers, one pulse.

In My Dream a Woman

answers the telephone,
she has round black eyes, floppy ears
matted yellow hair, a tail trailing
the hem of her dress.
 Will that be one pup or two?
 Small, medium, or large?
 Pick-up or delivery?
I give her both my addresses
hang up the pay phone
open my eyes as morning
begs me to rise 'n' shine.

In

I've said I'm sorry. I didn't mean to rush you.
What can I do to patch things up?
Love you.

Sent

You can give me more time.
I thought I was ready for commitment
but I'm not.

In

*Please just accept the ring as a gift
from me to you.*

Sent

You're moving too fast for me.

In

Is there someone else?

Sent

Yes, Tara and Millie.

Classified

I know where to find puppies for sale,
read the Classified Ads like a teacher
marking papers, a sharpened red pencil
between my fingers, give myself
points for learning
pups cost more than a jam jar full of loonies,
apartments for rent speak a code I've cracked:
n/p means no pets, no pups, no point
arguing with the landlord.

And something else, something
for bonus points:
photos of dead people decorate skinny columns
about their life and death.

I clip an example for Jimmy,
wonder if we might write an obituary
for Puffin, post a photo so no one
forgets the pig
we classified as loved.

Lady in a Red Plaid Shirt

I didn't yell HOLY TOLEDO!
for no good reason
yank my bike hard left
signal Jane to speed-demon
down 31st Street
race the lady
I saw step out from the alley
red plaid shirt, leash in hand
brown dog, four white socks
I didn't yell HOLY TOLEDO!
for no good reason
because I knew
those liquid black eyes
I knew that scar on its neck
HOLY TOLEDO! I knew
I knew that dog was Slim.

Mrs. Red Plaid Shirt

You had your suspicions?
Her appetite was voracious?
(Sure I know what that means.)
Her teats were swollen?
You felt her fat tummy?
She gave birth in a coat closet?
The middle of the night?
Every towel in your house?
Eight? Crazy Eights!
Each one the size of a tennis ball?
When did their eyes open?
You live across from the park?
The big pink house?
Your name is Irene Tootoosis?
Me?
Jane, too?
Can we bring our friend Jimmy?

Not Fair

Staged a hunger strike while Dad slapped together
    grilled cheese, chicken noodle slurp.

Chewed on him to move somewhere anywhere that
    allows DOGS.

Kicked Tara under the table for telling me to grow up.

Dried the dishes with the cuff of my best argument —
    divorce sucks.

Slam-boomed the bedroom door.

Fisted my pillow, punched the landlord's nose until
    it bled feathers.

Stood in the shower and rained.

Flock of Friends Overhead

If for a moment Jimmy wasn't all fidgets and thumbs
he could craft origami, it's easy-peasy-lemon-squeezy
but he prefers to squat on the art room floor, jiggle his
knees hum bouncy tunes, cut white paper squares for
the class, measure snip snip snip as everybody folds
in half, folds along the line, opens one flap *it should look
like this* folds the top triangle, folds the fold,
opens inward, flips, *whoops!* folds upward, presses,
folds downward, spreads the wings for our Japanese
pen pals, one for every student in our sister school,
their names printed in fine black ink along the slender
necks that Jimmy threads with invisible fishing line,
climbs a ladder, hangs twenty-eight symbols of long
life and happiness folded inside the tiny heart
of cloud-light, white paper cranes.

Thank-you Gift

What's in the box?
I can hardly wait to show you, Billy.
Why do you sound breathless?
I ran here; Mrs. Tootoosis said four o'clock.
The lady with the dog?
She's the best.
A gift for the pups?
Guess again
Dog cookies?
Cold.
A bone?
Colder.
A squeaky toy?
Frozen.
I give up.
Look!
Do they fly?

Irene Tootoosis

smiles with her eyes, feathery lines winking
as we follow her to a back yard
necklaced with mud puddle gems,
tufts of cloud floating upside down,
and in the middle, a crooked dog house,
diamond-shaped window to catch the sun,
TÂN'SI, stenciled across the roof, *tan-see*
she says, *my people's friendly greeting*.

Mrs. Tootoosis – *call me Irene!* whistled
two fingers, a quick command
as we leaned against the fence—
Jane, Jimmy, me
our eyes fixed on the dog house door,
a grey wool blanket
waved like a stage curtain
as a black nose poked around the side,
sniffed the cool air, *Tân'si*,
her black eyes blinking in the glare of visitors.

My feet bounced inside my boots,
Here Tân'si!—shook her head and floppy ears,
sleep-walked over to Mrs. Irene, tail wagging
hello hello hello, wolfed a biscuit
from Mrs. Irene's hand, jaw crunching

as we three stared
at the mud-caked hem of the door,
held our breath and waited for more
black noses, eyes, ears, tummies, tails,
Tân'si times eight friendly greetings.

Photo Gallery

Hung out with the computer
my mouse sniffing for cheese
a message from Jane:
Subject: *Puppiness*,
digital visuals dispatched pronto.

I hit print, fed glossy paper
until the ink ran dry, skipped
downstairs with one set of pix
for our bulletin board,
another for Dad—

Photo #1
Tickly on my cheek,
the rough tongue of *Tân'si* girl;
appetite for love.

Photo #2
Runt of the litter,
cradled in Jimmy's two hands;
asleep in a nest.

Photo #3
Triplets at the door,
three golden yellow sisters;
trio of good luck.

Photo #4
Arms linked like a chain,
we're best friends for always;
Jimmy, Jane and me.

Photo #5
For Mrs. Irene,
eight white origami cranes,
good luck in the air.

Thunderhead

Deep asleep when a voice
cracks the dark,
electric thunder in a nightmare field,
Mum standing scarecrow still
at the foot of my bed, the phone
clutched in her hand.

WHO IS IRENE TOOTOOSIS?

I rub my eyes in the hard glare,
but the tightness in my chest
suggests Mum knows the answer.

It's not fair, I say, sitting up in bed.
You had a dog when you were a kid.

WHAT DOES SHE MEAN YOUR PUPPY?

I kick back my blankets, yell
BUSTER GOLDIE TIPPY ROVER ROGER
MEGS BUDDY FLOYD SUZANNA.

Mum steps forward,
I duck my head
but her eyes clear from storm to first light
as the farm dogs from her girlhood
leap through her memory: *buster goldie tippy rover*
roger megs buddy floyd suzanna—

Remember? I ask.
You forgot Jackson, says Mum.

She sits on the edge of my bed,
tells me she has news from Irene Tootoosis:
The runt of the litter——your puppy——opened her eyes today.

In

Hi Mum! Jane has her very own cell phone!
Can I have one?
Love u.

Sent

When pigs fly.
Love u 2.

Tara Says Not to Get My Hopes Up

But it's too late.
I'm a hot air balloon
sailing high
pup in my arms
held tight as my hunch
Mum and Dad are in love again.
Why else meet for lunch,
go for dinner Sunday night
the two of them
alone?

Done Deal

Okay sure yes absolutely you bet
anything you say right away
practice piano scales every day, love
to run my fingers up and down
the deal I made, no complaining
about the weeks pup stays at home
no whining, wouldn't cross my mind,
no bad moods, who me?
Nothing I'd rather do than scrub
toilets, empty the garbage
make my bed, I adore a tidy room,
display an attitude of gratitude,
twenty-four seven I'm in heaven
thanks Mum, thanks Dad you guys
rock my ever-lovin' world.

Hold with Two Hands

Picking a pup is worse than first choice
at an ice cream bar.

Chocolate? Butterscotch? Or the runt whose paws
are vanilla dipped?

I've tasted all eight flavours of pup, kissed the tops
of their sweet heads.

They're dessert, treat, good medicine; the slow melt
down my throat.

Strawberry pink tongues, cocoa eyes, sugar scoops—
whoops!

I Drove to the Lumberyard with Mum

Bought wood, nails, paint,
we're building a dog house,
sawing, hammering, prepping
two-by-fours in the backyard.

Tara and I dipped our brushes,
played the name game.
Spring, she said, starting the volley.

Mum called, *Robin, Puddles, Lilac*.
Tara chirped, *Daffodil, Honey Bee*,
as I swirled *Sunshine*
in my can of white paint,
heard Billy offer *Halo, Cricket, Angel*.

Mum Behind the Wheel

Dad in the passenger seat,
(or so I imagined)
both of them together,
(for always, forever)
his apartment empty
(I wish, I wish),
beds sold, dishes donated
(gone for good)
to the Sally Ann.

But Mum didn't stop at Dad's apartment,
invite him along to visit the pups
drove directly to Mrs. Irene's house,
    house of *Tân'si*,
    house of eight *acimosisak* where Jimmy, Jane and I
    are her hungry *piyêsîs*, little sparrows,
    eating hot buttery bannock,
    mahti, we say in Cree, *ay-ay*,
all my made-up, invented imaginings
impossible as a foreign language,
the word *family* a tongue twister.

In

Hi Mum!
We're at Jimmy's house.
Can I stay for supper?

Sent

Did you practice piano?

In
Forgot, sorry sorry sorry.
Be right home.

Growing Pains

Holes in the knees of my jeans,
running shoes pinch but I don't care.

All I want is a name that fits
not too loose, not too tight.

Mum insists we shop bargains
for me, designer discounts for her.

I paw the merchandise, sniff
Calvin, Klein, Nike, Oscar, Hugo.

Arrivals and Departures

Grandma arrived last night by dog coach:
a Greyhound bus, its belly cargo-stuffed.
Mum, Tara, and I crowded the platform, waved
at Grandma through a stink-cloud of diesel fog
but as she stepped down and into Mum's outstretched
arms a shadow fell across Grandma's face and
suddenly I saw two children from a broken home,
divorce as real as the arrival of a bus from Winnipeg,
PLATFORM NUMBER FIVE.

Good Fortune

Every morning Grandma sweeps
Tara's hair into a topknot
while I wait for braids,

three thick strands in her hands—

one for luck,
one for love,
one for happiness.

my braids swinging, chickadees
dee-dee-deeing
as I fly out the door.

Rise and Shine

i)
Bells ringing inside my dream,
ding-dong, ding-dong, ding, ding, ding
bicycle bell, school bell, church bell
door bell, ding-dong
my bare feet on the floor
nightgown tripping downstairs
where is everyone?
rubbed my eyes, ran to the front hall,
ding-dong
peeked through parted curtains
saw Mrs. Irene on the front step,
red plaid shirt, arms empty.
She looked at me, grinned and pointed,
sun bouncing off the roof of her truck.

ii)
I dizzied the house caroling,
 puppy's here!
found everyone outside acting
normal as Saturday:
Grandma waved red rhubarb at me,
said she'd roll pastry for pie,
I yelled, We've got bigger fish to fry,
Mum stood up from planting peas,
Tara stopped dribbling the basketball
as the gate swung open wide.

iii)
Her size had doubled, milk teeth sharp
as needles, a wet black nose.
Grandma cradled her for a wiggly second,
Tara kissed the warm top spot between her ears
Mum scratched her tummy, set her down,
let her chew a blade of grass,
all I wanted was to squeeze her,
a golden loaf of bread,
tail wagging fast as talk.
Anybody home? Dad's voice at the gate,
my puppy, our puppy, a family dog.

iv)
Grandma and Mrs. Irene cooled themselves under lilac
shade,while Mum, Dad, Tara, me, formed a grass circle,
pup in the middle, our legs crossed at the ankles,
knees touching, skin and bone fence.

On the End of a Leash

Grandma weeds the lettuce patch
as I stand holding the leash, its pull
the tug of a question Billy asks:
Which name?
Our pup named herself.
How?
She sniffed moist dark soil in the garden,
found shade under a rhubarb leaf
a cool green tent
big as an elephant ear.

So what did she call herself?
Rhuby!

Our House has Insomnia

Wide awake lights burning
most of the night as one of us works to settle Rhuby,
her bed a cardboard box in the kitchen. I rock her,
baby her, set her down as both eyes close,
tiptoe back upstairs to sleep but no sooner is my light
dark when she whimpers, cries, lonesome yelps
wakes the house. Pajama Grandma takes a turn
then Mum in her nightgown, Tara stumbles
down for a shift, lights blinking the kitchen, bedrooms,
hallway, until sunrise makes us realize
we've been up all night, and Rhuby, by morning,
is settled and sleeping like a pup.

Backyard to China

I never knew a pup was so much work,
the attention she needs—
training, supervision, games of fetch,
walks in the park, before and after dark.

Mum doesn't have time to help,
she's got lessons to plan, papers to mark,
house to clean, the garden, groceries,
laundry, a list she recites
every time I return home from Dad's,
ask why she ties Rhuby in the backyard,
leaves her alone to dig holes
all the way down to China.

Memory Work

Yesterday Rhuby fell asleep in my lap,
one front paw patched over her eye

the other tucked under her rabbit-soft chin.
I petted all my favourite parts:

satin ears, velvet tummy, pink and black
marbled toe pads—each one a pearl button,

tiny sweat glands on her feet,
my hands memorizing the softness of pup.

Housebreaking

Rhuby should know better by now,
five months old but she still pees
on the living room carpet, jumps
on furniture, chews, bites, munches
anything, everything.

Mum covered the couch with clear plastic ugly,
spread newspaper across the floors,
bolted baby gates between doorways,
wound chicken wire around wooden table legs,
chair legs, hid shoes, purses, backpacks
gloves on the hat shelf.

We've got a dog that jumps on counters,
barks at strangers, cries in the night,
slobbers everything in sight,
our home a funhouse that isn't.

I Hate To Admit It

I miss Rhuby when I stay at Dad's but
NO DOGS ALLOWED is a sign that gives me a break
from cleaning up dog poop, dragging
Rhuby around the park on a leash, her straining,
me training her to *come*, *heel*, commands
she ignores no matter how much I yell,
offer cookie treats, wonder how other people
have dogs that obey.

Heart to Heart

Billy, did I make a mistake adopting Rhuby?
Maybe.
A guinea pig isn't as much work.
Guinea pigs die.
Everything dies, Billy.
Tell me something I don't know.
Sorry, it's just that I thought—
You hoped.
I hoped a pup would fix everything.
Mum and Dad?
Bring them back together.
Like a story with a happy ending.
Sort of.
I don't think that families work like stories.
What's a family, Billy? I don't know anymore.
I'm part of the family even though I don't live with you.
What's that supposed to mean?
It means you love me and I love you.
I guess I better think about that.
Think with your heart.
Billy, sometimes you talk like a riddle.

Careful What You Wish For

Mum invited Dad to the house for a *family meeting*,
her fancy term for dessert eaten in the living room,
Rhuby chewing a ball, the four of us polite
as strangers balancing plates of chocolate cake
on our knees, forks nibbling,
tea cups waiting for conversation to begin.

The sight of Mum and Dad together again,
opposite chairs in the same room,
gave me the heebie jeebies,
maybe Mum will finally tell us their split
is a red X on the test
of these last months.

I willed words for them in the hush,
apologies, forgiveness, hugs all around.

More cake?

But Dad barely touched a crumb,
didn't look at Mum or me or Tara, kept
his eyes on Rhuby, cupped her head in his hands,
finally spoke—*Cancer.*

Dark Shadows

Tara and I went back to Dad's apartment
kept him company, tried not to notice
his surgery date circled on the calendar
for next week, *a cancer that attacks
fathers, grandfathers, men.*

Our Dad, his disease a shadow
roaming room to room to room,
stealing the light.

Mount Patterson

I held the bed blanket like a sail for Tara,
let her climb aboard my boat
her tears falling, an ocean we drifted
into a dream about Dad,
his hair grey as smoke,
a long white beard, and a walking stick.

Come morning,
my stowaway called me *bed hog*,
scratched her head and said:
Our old man has a mountain to climb,
let's go with him.

Tender Loving Care

An entire school day
to remove a gland laced
with cancer,
Dad unconscious,
unable to feel needles
or the surgeon's knife.

He didn't open his eyes, slept
through the squawk of metal carts
rattling up and down the hall, shrill voices
on the intercom calling *Dr. You-Who*,
Dr. Hurry-up, *Dr. Move-It-Or-Lose-It*.

A nurse inspected plastic tubes
travelling from veins in his arms to bags
full of clear liquid
hanging like lungs
from metal stands, checked
his charts, smiled at us.

Take good care of him.
Lots of rest and fluids, no heavy lifting
for six weeks, plenty of TLC.

Down the Hall

I've moved again, not back to Dad's
but down the hall and in with Tara, packed
my jeans, sweaters, PJs,
alarm clock, hairbrushes,
vacuumed dust bunnies out from under
my bed so Dad can sleep at our house.

Mum insisted (hands on hips) that we swap,
double-up, trade bedrooms with her
behave like private Nurse Nightingales.

So now I share a double bed with Tara,
Mum across the hall from Dad
who calls for water, *please*
pills for pain, coffee black as the wet nose
that tickle-sniffs his big bare feet
ten little piggies and one tongue
pink as ham.

Homecoming

I tell Jane lies,
white as hospital bed sheets,
Styrofoam cups, skim milk,
the skin at Dad's wrist
where he wore
his watch,
    pale white lies
My Dad's home forever
even though I know my true colours.

Sous Chef

Carrots, potatoes, turnip, peeled and diced,
sliced onions that make me rub my eyes and cry,

chunks of chicken fried in olive oil, garlic.
Dark golden broth, veggies swimming,

the pot lidded to let our recipe simmer all day
until Mum thickens it later with flour, mixes

a paste that magically rises, a cloud
of dumpling she serves with stew to our patient.

Dinnertime aromas drift upstairs.
Strong hands prop him up in bed, pillows,

warm face cloth, hair combed, clean pajama top,
red napkin tucked under his sandpaper chin.

Question Without an Answer

Dad called me into his room
before I left for school, my eyes a road map
from getting up in the night twice with Rhuby,
Mum and Tara can sleep through her whines:
I can't.

Dad had shaved, was dressed,
sweatpants, his old blue shirt.
Sat in the rocking chair
near the window, a book in his lap
his eyes on me:
Who's training whom?

Listen William (Billy), Please?

Is it possible
to feel my finger trace
the stone letters
on your headstone?

Is it possible
to see the W in William
turned upside down
becomes the M in Millie?

Is it possible
for me to stand on my head,
see my troubles
from a different angle?

Is it possible
for you to take your upside down
troubles to the woman who knows
puppies from the inside out?

Ragged Heart

Tân'si, says Mrs. Irene, *come in, come in, I've just made tea*. I follow my friend into her bright kitchen where a dozen bread loaves are cooling on the counter. The scent of cinnamon and raisins makes my mouth water but all I can swallow are tears. *No thank you*, I say as she offers me a fresh slice. She takes my chin in her hand, lifts my head so that our eyes meet. *Ah*, she says, *Rhuby?*

Mrs. Irene knows my troubles the way she understands the mystery of a cinnamon swirl inside a loaf of bread. She pulls two chairs out from the table, sits beside me, pours tea as my words spill like a china cup overflowing.

Everything's broken, I sob. *My family, my puppy*. I can't fix anything. Suddenly she picks up her cup, throws it against the wooden floor. I jump but Mrs. Irene doesn't move. *Things break*, she says. *Not people.*

I kneel down to pick up the pieces, study a shard in my hand shaped like ragged heart. *Where do you go when you're home by yourself?* she asks after a few quiet moments. In my mind, I see my bed at Mum's, my bed at Dad's, the pillows, books and blankets that wait for me like trusted friends. Maybe Rhuby needs a space to call her own, I think. But she hates her dog house. She cries when we leave her outside.

Come, says Mrs. Irene, *I wonder if I've got an extra dog crate downstairs. Rhuby wants to live and sleep with you and your family because you're her pack.*

Brilliant. Why didn't I think of that? *Ay-ay*, I say, thank you, *ay-ay*.

Something Wrong

Rhuby doesn't greet me at the front door after school,
charge my knees, tug-bite my shoelaces.

I call but she doesn't come. Whistled
but who am I kidding?

I drag my backpack through the house,
kick a chewed slipper across the kitchen,
stop when I hear Dad's voice
from the back porch, run to find him standing
over Rhuby, feeding her biscuit,
telling her *good girl*. I stand still as stone, watch
them practice a routine that looks like wizardry:
sit
down.

Positive Negative

Eggrolls, ginger beef, pineapple chicken,
shrimp fried rice, a small feast
Dad ordered last night,
because of a surgeon's phone call
the report negative.

The sweet 'n' sour taste in my mouth confused me.
Why a table spread with celebration for a bad report?

Dad clinked water glasses with Mum, winked at Tara,
me, told us that *negative* means no more cancer,
no cells escaped the surgeon's knife.

I didn't know we were waiting for news
from the hospital
but I volunteered to phone Grandma,
tell her about the report that earned us
take-out food, good fortune cookies.

In Training

Our patient is patient with our impatient pup,
scamp, scoundrel, trouble-maker,
she's turned into a law-abiding citizen,
who pees in a backyard patch,
sleeps through the night in a crate
I lined with old beach towels,
a sleeping bag and the silver lining
Grandma told me to watch for,
a magic blanket woven from the soft
breath of a thousand wishes.

Basic Commands

sit come down stay leave it
come down stay leave it sit
down stay leave it sit come
stay leave it sit come down
leave it sit come down stay

biscuit biscuit biscuit biscuit biscuit

Facts

No cancer.
No chemotherapy.
No playing hospital.
No patient down the hall.

Four Plus One

We help Dad carry suitcases to his car,
nothing heavy for several more weeks,
pack his house plants, books, laptop computer,
the classified section where Tara
circled vacancies—apartments closer to home
so we can walk a block with our backpacks,
bring friends to Dad's apartment,
our apartment.

Mum stands at the curb with Rhuby on a leash,
Doesn't lean over, kiss Dad
goodbye.

Instead, she invites him to dinner
anytime or for Sunday morning
waffles golden crisp,
the four of us,
plus one.

Spring into Summer

Halo, hello, Billy.
Rhuby's here with me, off-leash
sniffing for graveside news.
Worried? Me? Not a chance.
She comes when I call.

She's seven going on
fourteen, get it?
I baked her a birthday cake
hard as milk bone
and she ate every crumb,
licked my face
when I hugged her.

This time next year,
you, me, Jimmy, Jane and Rhuby
will all be teenagers.

Hey, you're right, Billy—Rhuby
will be 2 years x 7 equals 14
in dog years
but all of us will be 13.
Guess that means
she'll always be leader
of our pack.

Billy, I've got more news:
we're going canoeing up north
for a week with Dad.
Get this: Mum's coming, too.

At Rhuby's birthday party
she and Dad told us
the holiday doesn't mean
they're getting back together.

Ya, that's what I asked.

Mum says it means we're
packing the blue tent for her,
the yellow tent for Dad,
and the red tent for me, Tara
and Rhuby.

What do you think, Billy?

Three tents, two canoes, one pup
sounds like a family.

Here Rhuby! Good pup.
Come, stay.

Acknowledgements

It takes a village to write a book. My thanks to Linda Stanviloff (now retired) from the Saskatoon Public School Board for arranging to workshop this manuscript with classes at Brunskill and Lawson Heights Elementary Schools. Special thanks to teachers Tammy Gordon-Dirks, Denise Rossmo-Wiegers, Trish Thurgood-York and their enthusiastic students.

Thank you to the folks at Coteau Books: John Agnew, publisher; MacKenzie Hamon, publicist and Susan Buck, typesetting.

Many people read and supported early versions of the manuscript. Thanks especially to Barbara Almas, Laima Cers, Barbara Kahan, Shelley Leehdahl and Kim Newlove. Thank you, ay-ay, to Naomi McIlwraith for advice on the use of Cree. Alice Major, my editor, provided intelligent and sensitive guidance.

Love and thanks to Randy, Rachel, and Anna for permission to share one of our favourite family stories—the naming of a little golden pup.

About the Author

Katherine Lawrence is a writer whose award-winning poetry includes *Never Mind* (Turnstone Books), *Lying to Our Mothers* (Coteau Books), and *Ring Finger, Left Hand* (Coteau Books).

Her work has been honoured by awards such as Best First Book, Saskatchewan Book Awards; the City of Regina Writing Award, and the John V. Hicks Long Manuscript Award. Her poems have been anthologized in *The Best Canadian Poetry in English*, 2010 and in *Nelson English Grade 10 Academic Edition* and *Elements of English 12* by Harcourt Canada.

Katherine also writes stage plays, coaches emerging writers, facilitates teen writing workshops, and chairs Access Copyright Foundation. She lives in Saskatoon and is originally from Hamilton.

www.katherinelawrence.net

ENVIRONMENTAL BENEFITS STATEMENT

By printing this book on FSC-certified recycled paper,
COTEAU BOOKS
ensured the following saving:

Fully grown trees	Litres of water	Kg of solid waste	Kg of greenhouse gases
1.67	6 101.07	74.79	245.34

These calculations are based on indications provided by the various paper manufacturers.

 Manufactured at Imprimerie Gauvin
www.gauvin.ca

Printed by Imprimerie Gauvin
Gatineau, Québec